MW00904389

My Little House Book of Family

For Grandma Dunn

—R.G.

Illustrations for the My First Little House Books are inspired by the work of Garth Williams with his permission, which we gratefully acknowledge.

HarperCollins®, ®, and Little House® are trademarks of HarperCollins Publishers Inc. Illustrations were prepared with the help of Cathy Holly. My Little House Book of Family *Library of Congress Cataloging-in-Publication Data Wilder, Laura Ingalls, 1867–1957.* My little house book of family / *adapted from the Little house books by Laura Ingalls Wilder ; illustrated by Renée Graef. p. cm. Summary: Uses characters from Laura Ingalls Wilder's books, along with simple illustrations and text, to describe the family life of pioneers. ISBN 0-06-025988-4. [1. Frontier and pioneer life—Fiction. 2. Family life—Fiction] I. Graef, Renée, ill. II. Title. PZ7.W6461Myf 1998 [E]—dc20 96-34740 CIP AC 1 2 3 4 5 6 7 8 9 10 ❖ First Edition*

MY FIRST LITTLE HOUSE BOOKS

My Little House Book of Family

ADAPTED FROM THE LITTLE HOUSE BOOKS

By Laura Ingalls Wilder

Illustrated by Renée Graef

HARPERCOLLINS PUBLISHERS

Ma

Ma kissed them goodnight.
LITTLE HOUSE ON THE PRAIRIE

Pa

Pa brought out his fiddle.
LITTLE HOUSE ON THE PRAIRIE

Sister

Laura lived with her father and mother,
her sister Mary, and baby sister Carrie.

LITTLE HOUSE IN THE BIG WOODS

Brother

Nellie and her little brother, Willie, came bouncing in.

ON THE BANKS OF PLUM CREEK

Baby

Baby Carrie was already asleep.
LITTLE HOUSE ON THE PRAIRIE

Aunt

Aunt Docia's dress was dark blue.
LITTLE HOUSE IN THE BIG WOODS

Uncle

Uncle George blew his army bugle.
LITTLE HOUSE IN THE BIG WOODS

Grandma

Grandma was jigging.
LITTLE HOUSE IN THE BIG WOODS

Grandpa

Pa and Grandpa came from the woods.
LITTLE HOUSE IN THE BIG WOODS

Cousin

The cousins were told to kiss Mary and Laura.
LITTLE HOUSE ON THE PRAIRIE

Family

It was a happy family.
THESE HAPPY GOLDEN YEARS